Elisabeth, the Treasure Hunter

Elisabeth,
the Treasure Hunter

by Felice Holman

illustrated by Erik Blegvad

The Macmillan Company, New York
Collier-Macmillan Limited, London

For C. H. H. and J. C. H.
who know how to look for treasure

THE autumn wind had blown the people off the beach and given it back to the gulls and the terns. Along the shore, the tide had left little pools among the rocks and sand, and they reflected the fall sky coolly.

"Oh, look, Papa!" Elisabeth said. "The sky in the pool is full of starfish instead of stars."

"Quite true," said her father, looking into the pool. "Quite true." Then he gazed down the beach, following the line of brown seaweed and shells at the high-tide mark, letting his eyes take him way down the curve of the shore to the long jetty of rocks that went out into the water.

"There's nobody here at all," Elisabeth said, following his gaze. "Nobody, that is, except you and me, and that pirate out at the end of the rocks."

"What makes you think he's a pirate?" her father asked, looking out to the point where a man was fishing.

"Oh," Elisabeth replied, "he's only pretending to fish, you know. I've been watching him. He hasn't caught a thing. I'm sure he's a pirate, guarding his treasure."

"Hmmm," said Papa. "Do you think it is hidden on this beach?"

"Absolutely!" said Elisabeth. She looked at him closely to see the effect of her idea.

"Oh, well, in that case . . ." began her father.

"In that case, I think we should hunt for it," said Elisabeth.

"How would you begin?" asked her father.

Elisabeth thought for a moment. "Well, I'd take my shovel and dig, mostly," she said.

"Hmmm," Papa said again. "I wonder if that's quite enough? You and I have no experience in this kind of thing."

"Yes," said Elisabeth with a frown. "That's true. If we could only get some experience!"

"Perhaps we could have a practice treasure-drill and then we would be ready for the real treasure when we learn all the tricks. What do you think?"

The idea was outstanding! Elisabeth nodded vigorously and smiled with great pleasure.

"It's getting near lunchtime. Let's talk to your mother about this." Papa took Elisabeth's hand, and they started back over the sand,

climbed the sea wall, and then hurried down the road to the house.

As they entered the kitchen, Papa asked Mama, "Do you think you could pack us a treasure? Valuable, but not too valuable . . . in case we don't find it."

Mama looked confused for only a moment, and then she brightened right up and moved busily about the room.

"I can have it ready in five minutes," she said.

"Good," said Elisabeth.

"Fine," said Papa, with a hungry look.

They turned their backs and, in less than five minutes, Mama handed them a bright red, tin box.

"Don't get your feet wet," she said.

When Elisabeth and her father returned to
the beach, the tide was very low and a pair of
ring-necked plover, very elegant in their dark
necklaces, were picking their way daintily along
the shore, looking for something tasty.

"I believe," said Papa, "that the tide has
ebbed as far as it is going to today." He looked
at his watch. "Yes, right on the button! Low
tide."

"You mean you can tell what time the tide
will be low?" asked Elisabeth.

"Oh, yes," Papa said. "The tide is as regular and as reliable as clockwork. With simple arithmetic we can tell at just what minute the tide will be high and low each day. But look, who is that?" Papa turned his attention to the figures of an extremely tall man and a very small boy who seemed very busy out at the sand bar.

"From his height and the cut of his coat, I think that's Professor Eckleberry," Papa said.

Elisabeth and her father walked down to the edge of the water, waded through a shallow pool, and then walked out onto the sand bar where, amid the long grasses, Professor Eckleberry and the little boy were digging for clams.

"Good morning, Professor," Papa called out.

Professor Eckleberry stood up straight. His elegant, long black coat and the heavy, gold watch chain across his vest seemed to Elisabeth a strange costume for the beach. But she did not say so. She felt better when she looked at his feet. They were bare, and his trousers were rolled up to his knees.

"Ah, good day, good day," said Professor Eckleberry.

The little boy turned and stared at Elisabeth in a way that was serious but friendly.

"What's that you're doing?" asked Elisabeth.

"Clammin'," said the boy, digging in the sand with his bare toes.

"My grandson Charles and I are just digging a few clams to bring to Mrs. Eckleberry for lunch," the Professor said. "Watch!" He reached for a large stone and threw it down very hard on the wet sand. Immediately, a little fountain of water blew up into the air, next to the stone. The little boy fell to his knees and began to dig. There, just a bit below the surface, was a small clam.

"Why, he showed you where he was!" Elisabeth exclaimed. "Could I do it?"

"Of course," said Professor Eckleberry, bowing a bit. "Help yourself."

Elisabeth picked up a stone as large as she could lift and threw it onto the sand. Nothing happened.

"Either that wasn't hard enough or there's

no one home down there," said Professor Eckleberry. "Try again over there."

Elisabeth threw the stone down again. Immediately a thin fountain blew up into the air. "There he is!" she cried. She dropped to her knees and dug with her fingers. "And here he is!" She held up the clam. Then she got a little water in her pail and carefully placed the clam on the bottom of it.

"That is a soft-shell clam," said Professor Eckleberry, "but that's just a manner of speaking. The shells aren't really soft so don't try putting your finger in one that's partly opened. They'll nip closed on you. That clam dug himself into the sand with a special foot he has. The sand protects him from the waves when the tide is in."

"Professor," Papa said, "I wonder if you could be of some assistance to us?"

"It would be my pleasure," said Professor Eckleberry. "We've got all the clams we need."

"Well," said Papa, "we've come down here to hunt for treasure." He held up the red tin box.

Professor Eckleberry raised his eyebrows, and Charles looked up with interest. "I see," Professor Eckleberry said, and then he sighed. "So few people find real treasure. Of course, sometimes they just look in the wrong places for the wrong things."

"Have you ever found a real treasure?" Elisabeth asked eagerly.

"Often," Professor Eckleberry said. "Often . . . and always." And then he put his hand up to his chin and seemed to forget about Papa and Elisabeth.

"Of course, one of the best ways to find treasure," said Papa, getting Professor Eckleberry's attention again, "is to be sure there is one." He held up the tin box again.

"Mmmm," is what Professor Eckleberry said.

"So," Papa went on, "it occurred to me that you might find it convenient to bury it for us. And then," Papa reached into his pocket and brought out a pencil and a piece of paper, "if you could just sketch us a simple map of its location or scribble a quick clue, we would be most grateful to you."

Professor Eckleberry looked at the box. "Well, I suppose that could be done. Yes, I suppose so." He picked up the box and started off down the beach.

"We'll keep busy around here," called Papa.

"Don't let the pirate see you," warned Elisabeth.

Charles was already busy at the end of the sand bar. He picked up a handful of soaking wet sand and let it dribble through his fingers to form beautiful designs. Then he let other dribbles pile up into little castles. Then he dribbled little turrets and ramparts. "Very soon," he said, "the water is going to come and flood this castle." He picked up a small mud snail that was going by and put it on top of the sand tower. "You know what else?"

"No, what?" asked Elisabeth.

"We are sitting on the bottom of the ocean."

Elisabeth thought about this. "My goodness, you're right!" she said. "Why, all of this," and she swept her arm toward the dark line of seaweed at the high-tide mark, "will be the bottom of the ocean when the tide comes in."

A loud cry made her look up. A gull suddenly dipped down to the shore at the tide line, grabbed something in its mouth, and then flew up high over the beach and dropped the something on the stones below.

"What is he doing?" asked Elisabeth.

Papa said, "He's found something good to eat that has a hard shell on it—perhaps a clam—but he can't crack the shell himself, so he drops it from a height onto the rocks."

"There he goes again," said Charles.

"Sometimes he has to drop the same shell several times," Papa explained. "And sometimes another gull will steal it from him when it falls. Then there's an interesting chase to watch." The gull gave another loud cry.

"You know what the gulls call, don't you?" asked Charles, returning to his castle dribbling.

"No, what?" Elisabeth asked.

"They say, 'Cha-a-a-arles. Cha-a-a-arles!' Like that."

"Oh," Elisabeth said, "it must be nice to have all those birds calling you by your first name."

"Yes, it is, rather," said Charles.

Papa seemed a bit grumpy. "To tell you the truth," he said, "I always thought they were calling *my* name."

"What's his name?" Charles whispered to Elisabeth.

"Horace," said Elisabeth.

"Too bad," said Charles to Papa, "but they don't."

Papa frowned, but cheered up quickly as Professor Eckleberry reappeared at the edge of the sand bar, with a rather pleased look on his face and a little piece of paper in his hand. He gave the paper to Papa.

"This is the first clue," said Professor Eckleberry. "You'll find the others as you go. But," and he held up his hand in warning and looked at his watch, "they're only good for a little while —an hour or so."

"Why?" asked Elisabeth.

"Aha!" Professor Eckleberry replied, smiling a secret smile.

"Thank you for your help, Professor," said Papa. "Will you join us?"

"No, thank you, I can't," said Professor Eckleberry. "Mrs. Eckleberry is waiting for the clams. But perhaps Charles, here, would care for a bit of a treasure hunt. He might even come in handy on some of the clues. Very handy."

"Could he, Papa?" asked Elisabeth.

"By all means," Papa answered.

Charles picked the snail off the top of his castle and joined them.

"All right," Papa said, as Professor Eckleberry disappeared beyond the jetty, "let's take a look at the clue."

Elisabeth and Charles came over to look and Papa read:

Three rocks near one rock,
Masqueraders dwell.
From house to house,
From shell to shell.

Elisabeth looked puzzled. Charles looked thoughtful. Papa looked annoyed. "Oh, for heaven's sake!" he exclaimed. "I only asked him to make a little map. Well, come on! We might as well get going."

Papa led the way, frowning at the clue as he walked away from the sand bar. Elisabeth followed, carrying her pail and shovel. Charles brought up the rear, dragging the long clam rake his grandfather had been using.

"The only thing I can make of this clue," said Papa, "is that we will find something or other, in or near something, that is near three rocks, that are near one rock. Hmmm . . . well, that much is clear." He looked happier.

They walked along single file for a minute or so and then Elisabeth called, "Papa, look! There are three big rocks right down at the edge of the water!"

Then Charles pointed and said, "And there's one rock all by itself farther up on the shore."

Elisabeth and Charles ran down to the edge
of the water where the tide had exposed three
large rocks. The rocks stood like mountains about
a small pool of water–water that had belonged
to the sea and had been left behind by the tide as
it slowly left the shore. Now, for a little while,
it was a separate pool and, as Elisabeth and
Charles peered in, they saw a strange sight.

"It's full of snails," said Elisabeth, "and they're
walking around pretty fast."

Papa came up to the pool. "If they're walking around pretty fast, you'd better look at them again. The snails I know are very slow-moving."

"They look like snails," Charles said, "but they have awfully long legs."

"Aha!" said Papa leaning over the pool. "What you have discovered here is a very clever character called the hermit crab. And you're right about one thing. His shell once belonged to a snail. The hermit crab has no shell of his own, you see, and so he borrows, or sometimes steals one, from a snail and uses it for a house."

"He's only pretending to be a snail, then," said Elisabeth.

"Yes, I suppose you could say that," said Papa. "The hermit crab looks for a bigger shell every time he grows a bit. The shell he has now will get too tight for him, and then he'll have to find a new home."

Suddenly a bright look flashed over their faces.

21

"That's the clue!" cried Charles, hopping on one foot.

"That's the clue!" cried Elisabeth.

Papa whipped the paper out of his pocket. He read: " 'Three rocks near one rock.' Well, that's right, anyway. 'Masqueraders, dwell!' *Masqueraders?* Why, that's the . . ."

"That's the hermit crab!" cried Elisabeth. "He's dressed up like a snail!"

" 'From house to house,' " read Papa.

" 'From shell to shell!' " finished Elisabeth and Charles together.

"I used to have one for a pet," Papa said.

"Oh, Papa, I want to take one home!"

"Me, too," said Charles.

"Why, look at that!" exclaimed Elisabeth. "There's a piece of paper in the pool, partly hidden under a shell."

"A piece of paper!" Papa exclaimed. "That must be Professor Eckleberry's next clue."

Charles reached into the pool for the paper. "Look what happens when I touch the hermit crab," he said. And right before their eyes the crab seemed to disappear, slamming the door of the shell.

Papa laughed. "He uses his legs to make a door. Let's see the clue." He took the wet piece of paper from Charles.

"What does it say?" asked Elisabeth.

"It says," Papa frowned:

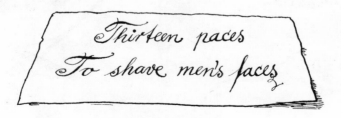

Thirteen paces
To shave men's faces

"That's all?" Elisabeth asked.

"Not another word," said Papa. "Now really! And it's way past lunchtime."

"Well, let's shove off then," said Charles. "Standing here isn't finding us any treasure."

"Exactly where would you suggest we shove off to?" Papa asked.

"Let's just mosey along the shore until we get an idea," said Charles, and he began to mosey.

"Wait a minute," Papa said suddenly, becoming his old cheerful self again. "It does say 'thirteen paces,' so if we're going to walk, we might as well count our steps."

Charles took the biggest steps he could, and

counted thirteen paces. Elisabeth counted her steps, but didn't get quite as far because she was walking behind Charles. Papa's paces took him farthest of all because his legs were the longest.

"All right now," Papa called, "let's each of us look around and see what he can see."

"I'm not a 'he,' " complained Elisabeth.

"That's just a form of speech," Papa said, stooping over to examine the wet sand.

"What I have is shells," said Elisabeth. "Hundreds and hundreds of shells! All shapes and sizes and colors. They're beautiful!" She sat down and picked out the shells she liked best and dropped them into the bucket. "This one looks like a doll's fan," she said.

"That's a scallop," said Papa. "Some of them have lovely patterns on them."

"And this shell looks like one of the turrets on Charles's sand castle," said Elisabeth, holding it up.

"It's a wentletrap," Papa said, "but some people call it the staircase shell. You can see why."

"And look at this one, and this one--and this one looks like a little boat with a seat in it."

"Then it won't surprise you to know," said Papa, "that it is actually called a boat shell." He turned around and called, "What have you found, Charles?"

"This crab," Charles said. "He just came out of a hole right at my feet. And look at him! His claws don't match."

Papa and Elisabeth went over to look. It was a strange-looking creature with one small pinching claw and one large one which he carried crossed over in front of him.

"Why, that old fellow is a fiddler crab," Papa said.

"Maybe they call him a fiddler because he

carries his claw like a violin," said Elisabeth.

"You're probably right," said Papa.

"And look at this one coming out from under the rock," said Charles. "He's green."

"He walks sideways," said Elisabeth.

"Ah!" said Papa. "His body is green, but he's called the blue crab. See his blue legs. Most crabs walk sideways, I believe. And they all have to change their shells from time to time in order to grow. These blue crabs just slip out of their old shells and wait for a new one to grow. While they're out of their shells, we call them soft-shell crabs."

"If they're out of their shells, they have no shells at all. Right?" asked Elisabeth.

"Right!" said Papa.

"Then why don't we call them no-shell crabs?"

"Well," said Papa, and there was a long pause. Elisabeth smiled. There was always a certain pleasure in asking Papa a question he couldn't answer.

"What I suggest," Papa continued, "is this. Let us walk very slowly, between Charles's position here and my position up ahead, and see if we can find whatever it is that will shave men's faces."

They formed their line again and walked along, heads down, looking closely at the wet sand.

"See that rock?" Elisabeth pointed. "It was uncovered when we were down here before, and now the water has come up over it."

"Tide's coming in," Papa said. "We'll have to hurry. Professor Eckleberry said the clues were only good for an hour, and I guess that's what his 'Aha!' meant. The tide will cover the clues pretty soon."

"Look at this funny, sharp shell sticking out of the sand," said Charles. "Oh, here's another."

"Here's another," said Elisabeth.

"Aha!" said Papa, stooping suddenly and pulling one out of the sand. "Aha!"

"Aha, what?" asked Elisabeth.

"These clams are called razor clams. See, this is one of the empty shells. It's shaped just like an old-fashioned razor. Now here's what I was thinking . . ."

"Razors!" exclaimed Elisabeth.

"Exactly," said Papa.

"Razors!" exclaimed Charles.

"Exactly," said Elisabeth.

Papa uncrumpled the wet clue. " 'Thirteen paces to shave men's faces.' "

"Well, that's settled," said Charles.

And then Papa said, "Well, I never!"

"What is it?" Elisabeth asked.

"Look!" Papa exclaimed. "I was just turning over this razor-clam shell in my hand, and there . . . do you see what I see?"

"There's writing in it," said Charles.

"It's another clue!" cried Elisabeth.

"I'm inclined to think so," said Papa. He looked closely at the shell, and read:

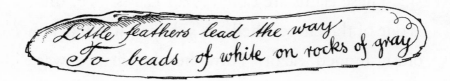

Little feathers lead the way
To beads of white on rocks of gray

Elisabeth said, "Papa, you're frowning again."

"Well, Eckleberry rankles me, that's all. No offense, Charles."

"No offense," said Charles.

"After all, this is my day off. I didn't expect to have to work so hard. And besides, I'm hungry."

"Charles and I can do this clue ourselves," said Elisabeth, taking pity on Papa. "Come on, Charles."

"Let me see the clue," said Charles, taking command.

"Can you read?" asked Elisabeth.

"Not actually," said Charles, "but looking at the writing helps me think."

Elisabeth and Charles stared at the clue as they wandered slowly up the beach.

"I'm getting hungry myself," said Elisabeth.

"I am, too," said Charles, and then he started walking in a way that reminded Elisabeth of a tightrope walker in the circus, putting one foot in front of the other and balancing with his arms.

"What are you doing?" she asked.

"I'm following the footsteps, see," he said.

Elisabeth looked down and saw the tracks in the wet sand.

"Gulls have made those tracks," said Papa, who would not be left behind, after all.

"They're very feathery footprints," said Elisabeth. "I'm going to take one home." And she very carefully took a bird track up in her shovel.

"Feathery!" exclaimed Charles. *"Feathers!"*

"Aha!" said Papa. "I think you have just discovered part of the clue."

" 'Little *feathers* lead the way . . .' " said Elisabeth, remembering the clue. "Oh, come on, let's follow them!"

They formed their line again. This time Elisabeth took the lead, holding the bird track on the shovel. Charles followed, carrying the pail. And in the rear came Papa, with Charles's clam rake over his shoulder.

The bird tracks led down the shore, right along the water's edge. In some places the water was lapping at the little prints.

"None too soon!" Papa said. "A few minutes from now the tide will erase these marks and spoil the clue. Old Professor Eckleberry was cutting it pretty close."

The trail led them right up to the stone jetty, and Charles and Elisabeth climbed up onto the nearest of the large rocks.

"The rocks are slippery," said Elisabeth.

"It's those reddish weeds that are so wet and slippery," said Papa. "They're called Irish moss."

"There's a pool of starfish in the weeds," Elisabeth said.

"That's the place they are most at home," said Papa. "A place that is wet most of the time suits

33

them best. Look at the rocks above us, and you can see the clear lines of color that mark the layers of rock, uncovered by the tide for different lengths of time. The things that need the sea the most live at the bottom. The strongest, like the periwinkles, live on the top because they have learned to live without the sea. The periwinkles are those small, brownish-gray snails. They live way up there in the crevices of the rocks, where they are covered only by the highest tides and wet by the spray. Below them are the layers of plants and animals that must be in the sea longer each day in order to live."

"The layer above us is all blue," Elisabeth said.

"Those are mussels," Charles said. "Grandpa and I sometimes gather them."

"There are so many of them," Elisabeth said. "What keeps them from falling off the rocks?"

"They make a little thread that holds them on tight," said Papa. "And they can move up the rocks a little at a time by making new threads."

"The layer above that is all brown seaweed," Elisabeth said.

"I see a white layer," said Charles, and he started to climb farther up the rocks and a little farther out on the jetty.

"Look!" Charles called. "The rocks are covered with thousands of little white cabbages. Ow! They're sharp!"

"They look like beads to me," said Elisabeth, who had followed him.

"Aha!" exclaimed Papa. "Beads! What kind of beads did you have in mind?"

"White beads," said Elisabeth.

" 'Beads of white,' " Papa said.

" 'Rocks of gray,' " Charles added.

"The clue!" cried Elisabeth. "The clue!"

"But what are beads doing here on the rock?" asked Charles.

"Well," Papa said, puffing out a bit as he did when he knew the right answer, "although these *look* like beads, or tiny cabbages, they are really a small animal called a barnacle."

"An animal!" exclaimed Elisabeth. "How can they be alive? They're so hard and they look so empty!"

"Some of them are empty," Papa agreed. "But many of them are closed up tightly over a little, upside-down animal that is waiting for the sea to come back. Many things on the rocks look different when the sea comes and covers them. The rockweeds float instead of hanging as they do now. Those blue mussels open up and start to

eat. The barnacles unfold and reach out of their shells, with their feet, for food, though they can never move from the place they have chosen to grow. They are fastened so tightly that even the wildest waves can't wash them away."

"There are barnacles on this rope, too," Charles said.

"Barnacles attach themselves to lots of things —even to the bottoms of ships," said Papa. "That rope is probably used to tie up a boat sometimes."

"There's no boat here now," said Charles and he tugged on the rope.

"But there is *something* on it," said Elisabeth,

and she went over to help Charles pull. "Maybe it's a fish."

"Not likely," said Papa. "Not likely."

Suddenly what was on the end of the rope came into view.

"Papa!" cried Elisabeth. "Charles! It's our tin box! It's the treasure! The treasure is tied to the end of this rope!"

And there it was . . . the tin box that Mama had packed. Charles and Elisabeth climbed down to the edge of the rocks, amid the red moss, and pulled the box out of the water.

"Why, that rascal Eckleberry!" Papa exclaimed. "The idea of putting our treasure in the water!"

"Maybe he didn't put it in the water," Elisabeth said.

"Maybe the tide came up over it," said Charles.

"Oh, let's see what's in the box!" Elisabeth cried, hopping on one foot and trying to pry open the cover at the same time.

"Here, let me help," Papa said. "There!"

Inside the box everything was dry as could be, and there was the treasure, looking absolutely marvelous! There were large chunks of gold, looking like beautiful peaches; pieces of jade and amethyst, looking like bunches of grapes shining in the sun; rare jewels, looking like red, yellow and green hard candies; and a great big piece of chocolate frosted cake, looking like a great big piece of chocolate frosted cake.

"Oh, Papa," Elisabeth cried, "of all the treasures we could find right now, this is the best!" She started to reach into the box, but stopped suddenly and held it out to her father. "Have some treasure, Papa," she said.

"Thank you," Papa said, taking a peach.

"Have some treasure, Charles," Elisabeth said.

"Thank you," said Charles, and he broke off a chunk of chocolate cake.

Elisabeth took a bunch of grapes, and they all sat down on the rocks to eat.

"Mama is really a fine treasure packer," said Papa, trying the cake. "Really fine!"

Elisabeth and Charles nodded, and sampled some of the jewels.

"Look down at the end of the rocks," Elisabeth said. "The pirate is packing his fishing things. If he goes away and stops guarding his treasure, perhaps we will be able to find it . . . now that we have the experience."

"Hmmm," said Papa.

"My feet are getting wet," Elisabeth said.

"The tide is coming in quickly now," said Papa. "We'd better be moving off the rocks," and he led them down onto the sand.

"But, Papa," protested Elisabeth, "we can't leave without the pirate's treasure. We've eaten the one we found, and now we have no treasure to take home."

Papa looked at Elisabeth, thoughtfully, and then at the pail in her hand.

"Oh, haven't we now!" he said, putting his hand into the pail and poking the hermit crab and the starfish and the periwinkles.

Elisabeth looked down at the pail. "Why, it *is* a kind of treasure, isn't it?" She smiled, and picked up the shovel with the gull's track on it.

41

Charles peered into the pail, too, where the mud snail from his castle was now settled snugly in the sand among the shells and seaweed. "Do you suppose *this* is what he was guarding?" Charles asked, glancing at the pirate.

"Perhaps," Papa said. "Perhaps not so much *guarding* as *watching*."

Elisabeth looked down to the point of the rocks where the terns were diving for fish and the gulls were screaming. She looked down at her feet, where the water was running back onto the shore, gathering in the little pools and all the creatures it had left for a while. She stamped very hard and a little clam blew her a fountain.

"And you know what?" Elisabeth said. "There's *lots* more treasure for next time."

DATE DUE	BORROWER'S NAME	ROOM NUMBER
NOV 5 2003	Ms Haney	K

FIC
HOL

1175

AUTHOR
Holman, Felice

TITLE
Elizabeth the treasure hunter

DATE LOANED	BORROWER'S NAME	DATE RETURNED
APR. 26	Paula Mang.	
OCT. 13	Lisa Mang	
NOV. 1	Maura Konaca	
	Rohl	4

Strange sounds from the marsh lead Elisabeth, Mr. Thew of the wildlife museum, her Papa, and her friend Stewart to an absorbing investigation.